ISBN: 978-1-950817-03-0 (Paperback)
ISBN: 978-1-950817-04-7 (Hardcover)

Any references to historical events, real people, or real places, are used fictiously.
Names, characters, and places are products of the author's imagination.

Front cover image by Milena Matić.

Printed by Power Corner Press, in the United States of America

First printing edition 2020.

Power Corner Press
1360 University Ave W Ste #351
Saint Paul, MN, 55104

www.powercornerpress.com

For Paige La'Nae Raino,
Who turned out to be a sister even more than a friend!
💕Hugs💕

Princess Paige loves lemonade;
it's sweet but tangy too.

She makes it with her Grandma
and shares it all with you.

With Daddy's help, she made a stand
as cute as it can be.

It has two hearts beside her name
and sparkly lights to see.

Mom walks Paige outside, where a shiny car awaits.
Inside, Dad is ready for their next lemonade date.

Paige likes to make folks happy,
that's why she cannot wait,

To get to her bright pretty stand,
she won't get there late.

"We're off to sell our lemonade!" Paige sings, her voice so fine.
At the stand, her fans are waiting patiently in line.
Young and old, they're waiting for a lovely cup.
Princess Paige does not wait long; she quickly fills them up.

A dollar here and a dollar there, business is just grand.
Who knew a girl could do so well with a lemonade stand?

Paige treats people like they're special, that's why they return.
As customers happily come and go, she's glad for all she earns.

When they finish at the stand, Paige and Dad go down,
to deliver their fresh lemonade in jugs around the town.

They drop off their delicious drink
to so many places,

and the people are so happy
to see their smiling faces.

Her goal for making money is to help children in need.
Mom and Dad are proud of her; they feel blessed indeed.

To have such a thoughtful daughter who loves kids so much,
That she makes her lemonade with an extraordinary touch.

While filling up another cup,
Paige tips another down.

It spills all over everything
and splashes on the ground.

The customers all draw a breath—will Paige get upset?
After all, her lovely stand has got sticky and so wet.

Instead of getting all upset, Paige looks up with a smile.
"Don't worry, I can clean it up; it may just take a while."

"Sometimes, mistakes happen."
Paige winks at her dad.
It's something that she learned from him
every chance he's had.

Paige and Dad count the cash
at the end of their workday.

All their things are packed,
so they go off on their way.

They're heading to the bank
to save their cash inside.

Princess Paige puts some in and puts some to the side.

The money that Paige puts aside she donates to sick kids.
Every time she helps someone, she's happy that she did.

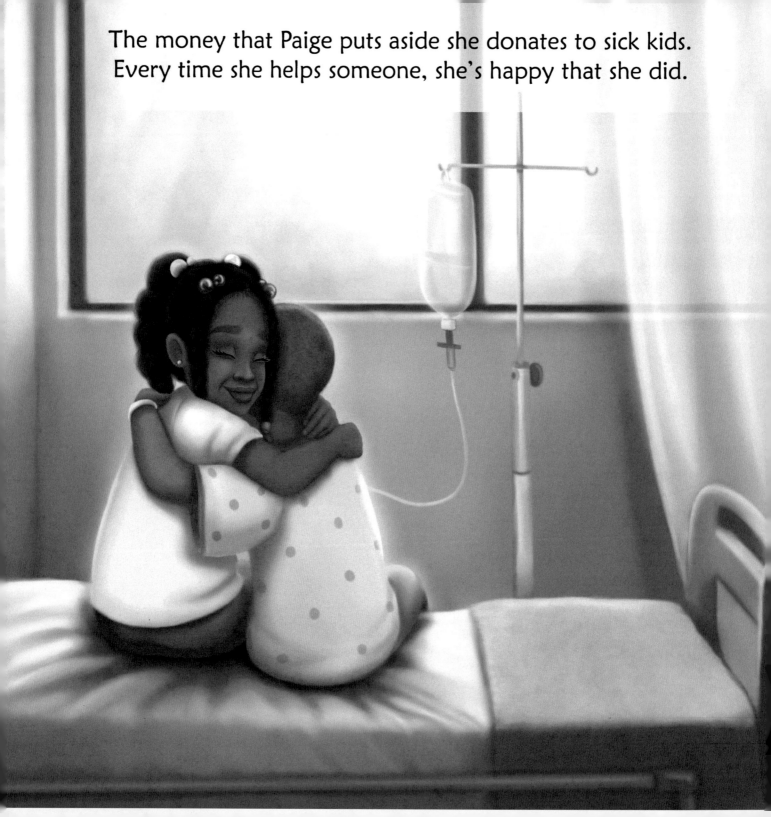

So, every summer Princess Paige serves behind her stand,
Earning and saving money for kids who need a helping hand.